GHOST PADDLE

GHOST PADDLE

A NORTHWEST COAST INDIAN TALE

WRITTEN AND ILLUSTRATED BY

JAMES HOUSTON

HARCOURT BRACE JOVANOVICH, INC., NEW YORK

HBJ

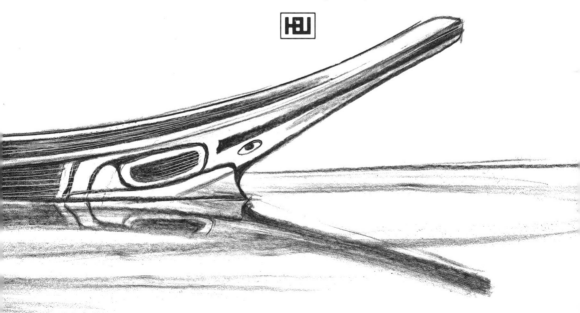

by the same author

TIKTA'LIKTAK: An Eskimo Legend
EAGLE MASK: A West Coast Indian Tale
THE WHITE ARCHER: An Eskimo Legend
AKAVAK: An Eskimo Journey
WOLF RUN: A Caribou Eskimo Tale

for adults
THE WHITE DAWN
ESKIMO PRINTS *(published by Barre Publishers)*

To Charles and Sylvia

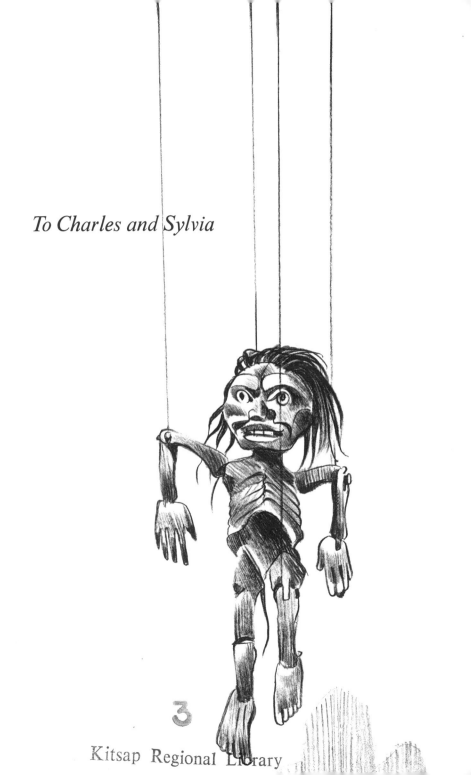

3

Hooits leaped up from his sleeping place and waited, crouching like a wolf. In his mind's eye he had seen masked hordes of sea raiders, swift paddlers, killers, lunging out of their canoes, clutching their heavy clubs and daggers as they overran the beaches of his island home.

He listened carefully. Had it been a dream, or had he heard real men shouting with voices almost hidden in the rolling thunder of the ocean's surf?

7

Shivering in the winter dampness, Hooits looked around the big Raven house. The fire in the center of this huge windowless room had burned itself out, but in the last faint glow cast by the red embers he saw his sister, Kaws-Kaws, sit up. She, too, was awake and listening, watching for any sign that he might give to her.

As he started toward the door, Hooits pointed to Kaws-Kaws, directing her to the long south wall where many cracks and knotholes were brightening with the coming of dawn. She left her sleeping place and hurried across the house, moving as smoothly as a wildcat creeping between the shadows. She peered out through the cracks, her sharp eyes searching the forest for any signs of attack.

Silently Hooits made his way past thirty sleeping Raven people before he reached the single entrance to the huge house. He found the strong man whose duty it was to guard the high entrance lost in dreams, squatting with his cape wrapped around him, his head resting on his knees. At least this guard had taken the precaution of pulling up the climbing log, but still, falling asleep was very dangerous.

Hooits bumped the guard with his knee, for he was ashamed of this man whose sleeping endangered everyone in this Raven clan house. No man or woman living within these walls could afford to forget that dawn was most often the time for enemy attack.

From the protection of the entrance hole Hooits and the guard stared out into the swirling gray mists. Sometimes Hooits glanced back into the big dark room, watching for any signal from Kaws-Kaws that would tell him if she had seen men moving in the forest behind the house.

At one moment Hooits was almost certain that he saw the shadowy figures of enemy warriors crouching on the beach near his father's war canoes. But as the morning light grew stronger, he could see that there was no one there, only his own fear and the drifting fog.

Hooits was a young prince of the Raven clan who had grown up in a time of war and raiding, a time of treachery and deceit. Fifteen winters had come to him since his birth, and during that time never once had he or any of his people dared to travel in the waters beyond sight of their island

9

stronghold. Wild anger and mistrust had come between the Islanders and the Inland River people, the fishermen who lived on the mainland beside the River of Eagles, and the Gwenhoots who lived to the north. The Gwenhoots were fierce night raiders, poor hunters, bad carvers, sly people who lived by their dagger points and fast canoes, and it was they who had started all the trouble. It now seemed to the young people that there was no escape, that their whole world was full of war.

Hooits wished that it could be a time of peace, a time when he could go sea traveling with his father, visiting distant people to the north and south, famous clans, princes and chieftains whom he could now only imagine. He wished that he could attend great potlatches, parties and gift-givings that sometimes lasted for half a moon or more, when proud young princesses of great dignity and wealth, wearing a fortune in shining abalone shell ornaments, sat on the priceless coppers and carved treasures of their families and called for the young princes of the Eagle, Raven, Wolf, and Bear clans to step forward and marry them. But with so much war, this could not be. Hooits was sad to think that perhaps he would never be able to leave his island home. Before winter came again, he would have to begin his training as a warrior.

Hooits turned away from the entrance and walked back into the huge room toward the morning fires that were now beginning to blaze. He heard two servants on the roof removing some of the wide planks to let out the cooking smoke.

The name Hooits means Grizzly Bear. It was a name that suggested strength and courage but was not well suited to the young prince, for grizzly bears are rough and heavy, bad-tempered and clumsy creatures. This young nobleman, Hooits, was lean and quick for his age, and it would have been better if he had been given a bird's name, perhaps Sea Hawk or Golden Eagle, to match his swift movements, his black feather-bright hair, but most of all to suit his hawklike nose and his dark, shining eyes. Hooits might also have been called Sea Otter, for he was sleek and brown and loved the sea. Or perhaps he might have borne the name of Mountain Lion, for he possessed within him a hidden spring of power and the quick, nervous energy of a dancer.

Hooits' father was named Wasco, the Sea Wolf. He had been a famous warrior of the Wolf clan, and it was said that not a braver man lived anywhere along the whole coast. Now Wasco was a white-haired chieftain who had grown old and wise.

This morning Wasco sat quietly beside the fire, waiting for food to be brought to him. Hooits went and sat beside his father, opening his cape to let the warmth of the fire drive away the winter dampness. He waited there, without speaking, feeling his cheeks burn red with the heat of the flames.

Wasco turned to Hooits and said, "Our morning fish is dry and tasteless. This war has lasted so long that you and Kaws-Kaws do not remember the rich flavor of fish cooked in the sweet oil of oolichan. I want this war to end now," he said, pounding his hand on his knee. "This war robs us of everything that is good in this life and causes us to sleep in fear."

"How can we end the war?" asked Hooits.

For a long time his father did not answer him, but sat deep in thought, his eyes fixed on the fire.

"Perhaps there is a way," said Wasco. "Perhaps there is a peaceful way, if you will help me."

That night the village clans were gathered in the Raven crest house, and when everyone was silent, Wasco, the Sea Wolf, rose to speak.

"You recall," he said, "the time when all of us were young and possessed canoes and warriors in equal numbers with the Gwenhoots. We were never their friends nor were we their enemies. It was then that the bearded men in white-winged ships came to trade only with us. They did not trust the Gwenhoots, for they had once fought a terrible battle with them.

"Remember our first pleasure in possessing the foreigners' bright mirrors, iron knives and kettles, and rum and blankets in exchange for the pelts of sea otters. We soon became rich and powerful.

"But, of course, the Gwenhoots grew jealous. They were obliged to come and trade with us because they, too, wished to have these rare things from the pale men. The Gwenhoots became like slaves to us. They were forced to bring us the ivory walrus tusks, raw green jade, and native copper that they had taken from the little kayak people in the far north. For these we also traded to the Gwenhoots some of our most beautiful wooden helmets, clubs, daggers, and hardwood armor.

"That was our terrible mistake. We would pay dearly for our greed in selling them such weapons. The Gwenhoots, those sea raiders, those thieves who grew so strong in cunning and weak in courage, sneaked over to the mainland, crept up the long trail beside the River of Eagles, and in the dark of night raided the villages of the Inland River people, capturing their women and children, stealing their precious boxes of oolichan, the delicious grease fish.

"Worst of all, those raiding Gwenhoots left scattered behind them our carved helmets and our weapons, so that the Inland River people, seeing the beautiful workmanship that had been lavished upon these weapons, would know that only our hands could have made them. Thus we were blamed for that treacherous raiding, and open war broke out between the mainlanders and ourselves. We are no longer welcome in any village along the whole length of the mainland coast. Even the distant sight of our long canoes causes the mainlanders to snatch up their children and flee into the deepest parts of the forest. This is wrong. It is unfair to them and to us.

"When the Inland River people became angry, they sent us a warning. They sent back our relative, the old Raven man Yahil, the man who had lost his right hand long ago before he married one of the River women and lived in her clan with them. They threw him secretly onto our beach one night during the autumn moon, and they told him to tell us that only when his hand grew back upon his wrist, could we resume our trade with them. They meant what they said. They were so angered by the wrongs they believed we had done to them that they wished never to trade with us again.

"After all these years, I know now that we must be the ones to go and search for peace. How better could we show our friendly intentions to the Inland River people than by having a few of us appear before them as a party of simple berry pickers, gentle traders of wood carvings, surrounded only by our young men and women. I know it will be difficult for Raven people to humble themselves in this way. But think of the little oolichan, those fish so oily that, when lit, they burn like the wax candles from the traders and make the winter lodges bright. The fat pressed from them makes the simplest seaweed taste delicious, turns every giant clam and salmon into a rich oil-soaked feast, and causes the toughest piece of wild goat meat to grow tender and melt in your mouth like honey. It would be nice to have the oolichan again."

The next morning when Hooits awoke, his father and the other warriors had already left the village. They were out watching the Gwenhoots, who were paddling dangerously close to the north beach, and when the tide was right, they rushed out in pursuit of them. But at midday the winter rains came and turned to sleet, and the sly Gwenhoots disappeared into the rising seas and fog.

When Hooits' father returned to the Raven house, he was so tired that he could not stay awake to eat. He fell into a deep sleep, and in the black of night many heard him call out loudly. They believed that he was perhaps remembering some violent sea battle of his youth.

In the morning Wasco was silent and went and walked in the forest alone, speaking to no one. He returned in the evening and called Hooits to him.

"Last night I had a dream," he said, "a dream that may have been a good or evil omen, I know not which. In this dream I saw you, my son. You were paddling on a ice-smooth sea in a small painted canoe. I remember now that the winter moon had a ghostly face and you were dressed as a simple fisherman, but you wore a tall chief's hat.

"Suddenly that smooth silver sea was lashed into violent waves and flying foam, as though a monster churned it, and I saw the paddle break in your hands. You gripped the sides of the canoe, and I saw you change. Your arms grew thick-

15

muscled as a warrior's arms and your body was covered with hardwood armor. Your face was hidden by a fierce fighting helmet; you wore a long dagger and carried a whalebone club. I could see that the waves would soon upturn your canoe and drown you. Still I lay sleeping, powerless to help you.

17

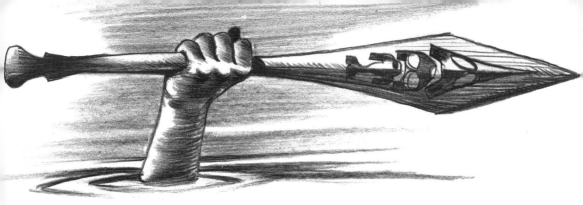

"Then I saw a magic hand reach up from the roaring sea and hold a paddle out to you. You took it and gave the waves one deep stroke, and instantly the sea grew deadly calm. Your warrior armor faded, and you once again wore the bark cape of a peaceful fisherman.

"I do not know the meaning of this dream, but the vision of that arm with the paddle raised above the waves is very clear to me. I can even now remember the exact design on the paddle blade.

"Tomorrow morning, if the wind is down, I shall search the western beaches. If I find the right wood, I will try to make you such a paddle. Imagine! I shall try to fashion a paddle from a dream, a ghost paddle."

All the chiefs of Eagle, Raven, Wolf, and Bear gathered in the crest house to discuss Wasco's plan for peace. They spoke to him and asked him to form a small peaceful party and to go to the mainland. But they warned him that such an unarmed journey into enemy country would be a very danger-ous venture and one that seemed to beg for a terrible revenge by the Inland River people.

Hooits' father raised his arms, and the roof boards above him were flung open to the stars. White eagle down scattered by some servants floated around him. This was the sacred sign of peace, the sign for which so many had waited. A joyous sound like singing rose and spread throughout the big room, so pleased were all the clansmen.

"When the canoes are ready for traveling and the food and gifts are prepared, we shall make a voyage to the mainland," said Wasco. "If you agree," he added, turning to the chieftain of the Wolf clan, "I shall take my son, Hooits, and your son, Hawn." Then facing the carver named Killer Whale, he said, "I would like to take your son, too."

Then to everyone he said, "Other young men are welcome to join us. Those who have not yet trained as warriors should come, for we go seeking only peace.

"If they wish to come with me, I will also take my daughter, Kaws-Kaws, and some of her friends."

A feeling of hope and excitement ran through all of the young people as they helped prepare the two big dugout canoes for the journey. The fierce clan designs of Raven, Wolf, and Killer Whale painted on the curved prows of the canoes were blackened out, for this was not to be a war party.

Their preparations of food and gifts for the voyage continued for half a moon, and during this time, Wasco carefully carved the ghost paddle. Finally it was finished, this paddle fashioned from a dream.

In the Raven clan house the fires were built high. The

19

whole of the clan gathered as Hooits stood before his father. The old Sea Wolf held the carved likeness of the ghost paddle out to Hooits and sang:

"Nexnox, Nexnox
 have pity upon him.
 Hold your breath, Nexnox,
 that it may be calm for him.
 Nexnox, Nexnox."

The name of the sky god was Nexnox. It was he who controlled the wind and rain. That is why Wasco asked him to hold his breath and protect his son. This was a very ancient song of the sea hunters. It was usually sung at sea, and Hooits had never heard it before.

When Hooits took the paddle from his father, it seemed to him that he felt the smooth shaft tingle in his hands. The next morning when he awoke, he slipped the paddle out carefully from its hiding place beneath the raised wooden platform that was his bed. The faint firelight caught its short, strong handle and its wide, thin blade.

The wood of the paddle was foreign. Wasco had found some wonderfully strange wood that had been washed up upon their beach from across the ocean. It was old and white as ashes, and the smooth grain of the wood flowed gently downward, curving from the shaft to the blade, running like ancient rivers of silver. This paddle was strong as iron, and yet it possessed the easy spring of a willow branch. Wasco had shaved the paddle's blade as thin as a knife's edge, and he had pointed it like a spear. This he had done with treasured pieces of broken trade mirror that had belonged to Hooits' mother.

Only when the paddle was smooth enough for a sea hunter to dip in and out of the water without making a sound, had Hooits' father painted it with charcoal black and berry red, both mixed with the sticky eggs of salmon. The whole blade was covered with bold decorations. The Sea Wolf crest could be seen cleverly entwined with those of the Raven and the Bear. Wasco had followed exactly the patterns he had seen in his dream, and he had waxed it with wild goat tallow until it was waterproof and ready for a journey. It gleamed in the last light of the fire. The crest figures on the blade seemed to move their dark eyes as though they possessed the very power of life itself.

That evening Hooits talked for a long time with his mother and then walked alone into the forest. He wandered aimlessly, listening to the ghostlike winds murmuring through the giant trees. He loved the idea of peace, but he did not know whether he had the courage to walk without weapons into the forest traps of the Inland River people, knowing that their hearts were filled with hatred, knowing that they believed his people had stolen their wives and children.

The next morning at dawn, to purify himself, to wash away his night fears, Hooits ate some bitter berries and ran naked into the sea. He stood waist deep in the icy water and scrubbed himself red with rough sand. Later he stood shiver-

ing on the cold beach, thinking, "I am not a warrior, but I must now try to gain the courage of my ancestors. I believe the paddle my father has made for me may have the power to calm the sea."

When his skin was dry, Hooits tied on his short loincloth and hunting bag and drew his woven cedar rain cape around his shoulders. He placed his hat of woven spruce roots upon his head and walked along the shore until he came to the very tip of the island. A flock of nervous sandpipers awakened, raced across the beach and took off, skimming low over the water, calling out to him, "Pee-ook, pee-ook," as they disappeared into the thick white fog of morning. The wind had died, and the whole sea was crystal smooth and still as new-formed ice.

An old totem pole called the Giant's Finger, which had been made for his grandfather before his marriage, had rotted in the heavy rains and toppled into the sea. It was so worn by weather that its carved figures had almost disappeared. When the tide was high, its tip still floated, pointing eastward to the distant cloud-hung mountains of the mainland.

23

Hooits made his way carefully out along the worn gray pole, and when he reached the very end, he sat down, cross-legged, between the ancient Raven's eyes. He drew his wind flute from his belt and waited, looking around for some sight or sound that would set his mood, would tell him what to play.

As Hooits sat thinking, a big humpbacked salmon rose lazily up through the water beyond the end of the pole and broke the smooth stillness of the surface with his rising fin.

Then slowly the salmon dove and broke the water once again with his shining tail. Hooits watched the two bright rings of water that spread in ever widening circles and placed the wind flute to his lips. He blew two long notes, one for the fin and one for the tail. Then he listened, as the haunting sounds echoed back from the mountains now lost in fog.

Another salmon broke the water's surface, and Hooits would have blown the notes again, but behind him he heard running on the beach. He heard his name shouted breathlessly by Hawn.

"Hooits! Hurry! Hurry! We are leaving for the mainland," Hawn called. "Run! The boats are leaving now."

Hooits jumped up, ran the length of the fallen totem, and leaped onto the sand.

Hooits and Hawn raced toward the village. Hawn, whose name means salmon, arrived first. He should have been called Deer, for he could certainly run like one.

They arrived breathless and saw that the first big canoe had already left the beach. As they ran for the second canoe, Hooits searched among the people who remained behind. He saw his mother standing between her brothers and her powerful cousins, all brave sea hunters who wished they, too, could go and protect their relatives. She raised her hands in farewell to his father and to Kaws-Kaws. Her face looked drawn and tired, as though she had not slept at all.

When she saw Hooits, she ran down the beach to hand him the ghost paddle that his father had made for him. Others, the clever carvers and many of his village friends, ran beside her, calling out encouragement, and joined in helping to shove the second boat safely out into the tide.

When the big dugout became free of the shore, Hooits and Hawn leaped in, and each took up his position for paddling. Wasco and Yahil were the only two persons who were not young. Each sat as a steersman in the stern of the canoes. Instead of masks and hardwood armor, they all wore ordinary garments of cedar capes, button blankets, and spruce-root hats. They carried no weapons; they had many gifts for trade.

Hooits felt some inner power of the paddle tingling in his hands as he dug it into the water for the first time.

"Hoi Woes! Hoi Woes!" shouted the people on the beach, calling for the southwest wind, the rain wind, to help the travelers on their journey.

"Hoi Woes. Hoi Woes," answered the boatmen as they set up a rhythm and with their eager paddles drove the two high-prowed dugouts seaward.

Beyond their protective inlet they reached the true sea, and the wind blew strongly. The two canoes raised small square sails, and the steersmen set the course. The long, slim dugouts seemed to fly across the water, trailing wide white wakes through the pale dawn.

Slowly the morning sky turned blue, and looking back, Hooits proudly saw his island homeland. Around its shores stretched high gravel beaches and a thick undergrowth of lush green brush. Above this stood the giant red and yellow cedars, and beyond them, at the very center of the island, stood the shining mountains, whitecapped and glowing in the distant haze, with cloud plumes streaming from their peaks.

Toward evening, the wind died. They paddled until dark. Then they lashed the two canoes together, binding their long paddles across the gunnels to steady the boats. They ate an evening meal of cold foam soup and sun-dried halibut. One by one the stars disappeared, and Hoi Woes, the wet wind, came at last. Lightning flashed across the dark Pacific, cutting through towering black thunderheads that rumbled across the ocean's face. The long, dark rolling of the sea made it a frightening, eerie place.

Hoi Woes spilled her rain in hard, driving sheets against the travelers. They huddled together, trying to sleep under their cedar rain capes, trying not to dream of the dreadful sea monsters they feared might swim beneath them.

In the morning the rain ended and the fog cleared. Raising their small sails once more, they set their course toward the blue peaks of the mainland. Long before sundown they could see the boiling white waters at the river's mouth and hear it roaring in the distance, for it was a time of full flood. Above the river, white-headed eagles soared on wide wings, wheeling slowly, searching the waters for their prey.

The next morning, after sleeping on a small island off the river's mouth, they journeyed to the south bank of the mainland. There they hid the two big canoes, then gathered all their boxes filled with their beautifully carved wooden masks, rattles, goat horn spoons and knives. They picked up a delicately decorated small canoe that they had brought inside the biggest boat, and inside this Hooits tied his precious ghost paddle.

Walking in single file, they started up the long path that led inland beside the roaring river. No one was without some feeling of fear. Each night when their march was done, they moved away from the river and went deep into the forest to camp. By bending down young saplings and flinging skins over them, they formed quick, crude shelters. Only then did they light their fires, burning nothing green, making as little smoke as possible.

Hooits and Hawn usually helped the one-handed old man, Yahil, to bend the saplings for his sleeping place and noticed that he was nervous and often looked quickly behind himself, as though he expected a surprise attack from the River people whom he knew so well.

On the fourth morning of their march, Wasco called Hooits and Hawn to him and said, "Did you hear that woodpecker hammering in the forest just at dawn? It was such a good imitation that I heard a real woodpecker give an answering sound. But the first sound was not made by any bird. It was a River man, an archer, signaling to someone else. At least two people watch us in this forest. They walk when we walk, sleep when we sleep, always unseen.

"We must move more quickly," said Wasco, "but I find it hard to set the pace. One of you must lead, dressed in my robes and headdress. This becomes a dangerous thing to do."

"I will do it," said Hooits.

"And I will do it tomorrow," said Hawn. "That way we will share the danger."

"As you wish," said Wasco, peering around, for like Yahil he did not trust this strange forest.

"It is now that an old warrior like myself longs for a canoe full of armed sea fighters to surround him like a warm cloak in winter. But it was our idea not to have them. There is nothing we can do except to go forward in peace. Do not tell the others about the bowman's signal, for there is nothing so frightening as someone who walks unseen beside you along the forest trail."

Feeling strange eyes upon them, Hooits and his father hid beneath some heavy bushes and exchanged their clothes. Hooits wrapped himself in his father's splendid goat-hair blanket and placed a Raven's frontlet on top of his head. White ermine skins richly lined with bright red trade cloth hung grandly down his back. Wasco, like all the other men, put on a simple cedar cape and carried one of the big boxes on his shoulder. Kaws-Kaws and the other girls still had the woven berry baskets strapped on their backs.

Continuing along the path beside the River of Eagles, they were suddenly confronted by a fresh rough-hewn plank of red cedar driven deep into the very center of their path. It was shaped like a gravepost. It was a very bad sign. On it was a crude black painting of Hamasata, the cannibal spirit that haunts the woods. This sign placed in their path was a warning to turn back. But Hooits walked bravely around it and motioned to the others to follow him.

That night the one-handed man, Yahil, heard a noise in the forest. He turned to Wasco and asked, "Was that not the sound of a man sharpening a dagger or an arrow's point against a stone?"

Yahil knew too well all these signs and secret noises of the River people, and he became so nervous that he wept.

Wasco spoke to Yahil. "You are right, old man. Tomorrow we must be careful. Death may come out of the forest.

On this fifth day of walking, Hawn rose early. In the gray mists of morning he opened the food box and ate cold fish with the chief, Wasco. They talked secretly together as they

ate, and when they were finished, they hid from view and exchanged clothes.

Walking bravely erect, in imitation of a chief, unarmed, and carrying only the talking stick before him, Hawn lead the Island people eastward. They stopped once to drink some water and to eat a few handfuls of berries. No one spoke above a whisper. They felt so sure of an attack that Kaws-Kaws had to urge some of the girls not to turn back to the safety of the canoes.

Just before evening, Hooits heard Hawn groan and was surprised to see him sink slowly to his knees. He wondered how he could tire so easily, knowing that he carried nothing but the chief's staff. Wasco and Hooits stepped forward to ask Hawn what was wrong. They reached his side just in time to catch him as he started to fall forward. At that moment they saw a black-feathered arrow protruding from the center of his chest.

Hawn fell to the ground. The Raven headdress tumbled from his head. Hooits gasped in horror. But in the fall, the chief's blanket was flung open, and Hooits saw the leather-bound slats of hardwood armor that Wasco had made Hawn wear hidden beneath the goat-hair robe. Hawn lay still as death to deceive any eyes watching from the forest, but Hooits saw a faint smile flicker across his lips and knew that the arrowhead had been turned and broken so that it did no harm.

Treating Hawn like a dying man, Wasco felt him all over,

then, weeping, covered his face with his blanket. Many helped to bear him away into the forest, and his body was placed beneath the small upturned canoe. When darkness came, the women sent up a mournful wailing, a crying suitable for the death of a noble chief. The women took turns doing this throughout the night of rain.

In the morning when the fog lifted, the party was ready to move again. On this day, Wasco himself wore his own garments. He called the two bearers of the small canoe to come

forward, and they walked immediately behind him, in front of all the others. Soon he called the frightened old man, Yahil, to join him, and then he beckoned to his son.

"We have almost arrived at the river crossing," he said to Hooits. "A few steps more, and if you look on the other side, you will see the first of their river village houses.

"Now is the time to ask the clever Raven of your mother's clan to help you. Now comes the time that will truly test your courage. Dare we go forward into this nest of arrows, clubs, and daggers unarmed and without help? Will you come with me?"

"Yes," answered Hooits.

The old man, Yahil, was trembling, but he, too, nodded his head.

Together Hooits and Yahil carried the little canoe forward, with Wasco walking proudly beside them. They came to the place where the path turned down to the river, and through the trees they could see the tall totems and the bold designs painted on the big Inland houses.

Right behind the canoe came Hawn and Kaws-Kaws. She tried to appear calm, but her face was pale. She was so afraid for her father and her brother that she pounded her thighs with clenched fists beneath her cape so none could see, and bit her lip until the blood came. Both she and Hawn believed that they would never see these three alive again, yet they dared not show fear.

The sun appeared weakly through the heavy rain clouds above their heads. Hooits looked across the rushing river at this Inland village, the first that he had ever seen. He saw many bright colors and the quick movements of warriors. The five River chiefs had banded together in their hunger for revenge, and now their fighting men strode back and forth, back and forth, proud in their rich robes and tall headdresses. Hooits could see many wild masks and war clubs and hardwood armor and bows, and a dozen newly painted war canoes standing ready to attack them if they tried to paddle across the river. Hooits heard singing and shouting and knew that the powerful Inland warriors were slowly working up their anger for battle.

Hooits wondered who else would ever be so daring, so madly brave, as his father, Wasco. Who else would have the courage to cross this rushing river in this little two-man cedar dugout and go against all the long fighting canoes and the terrible warriors of five villages? Anyone else, he thought, would order his people to return to the safety of the sea. But not the Sea Wolf.

37

After unlashing the ghost paddle from inside the canoe, Hooits felt a warm hand on his arm and heard his father say to him, "Show them your bravery by paddling this small canoe straight to the place where those chiefs now sit."

Quickly the Sea Wolf sat down in the center of the small canoe, and Yahil climbed nervously into the bow.

Hooits, wearing only the simple loincloth and twisted cedar collar of a paddler of the lowest rank, took his place in the stern and shoved the canoe out into the water. He felt the paddle tingling again; it did seem to have a power of its own. He stole one backward glance at his sister, Kaws-Kaws, for he was sure that he would never see her again. He saw tears glistening on her cheeks.

Hooits looked across the water at the hordes of Inland warriors and wanted desperately to leap out of the little canoe and run for his life, to disappear deep into the forest forever. He thought, "I am only a boy, a flute player, a singer, a dreamer, one who does not wish to be a warrior, one who is

too young, too untrained for battle." But he drew a deep breath, threw back his head grandly, and forced the small dugout canoe into the strong rushing current.

The bow was quickly swept downstream by the power of the river, and Hooits was amazed to see how cleverly the old man used his good hand and wrist stump to keep the front of the canoe in line. Hooits felt the dugout shiver, then shoot forward with each powerful thrust from the ghost paddle. It skittered like a leaf out into the center of the mighty surging river.

Together the five chiefs gave a downward hand signal, and with a rush a hundred powerful Inland warriors leaped into their waiting long canoes. As they drove their great war canoes out to meet the frail little two-man dugout, Hooits could hear them laughing with the thought of the sport they would have.

Old Yahil was trembling with fright, but he paddled hard and kept the bow of the canoe straight. Wasco looked back, for he could not believe that his son possessed the strength to paddle a canoe against the current of this mighty river or to guide it so cleverly.

As the many warriors paddled near, they began to sing a wild war chant, and Hooits heard his father, full of excitement, singing back to them. The little dugout passed between two mighty war canoes, and looking up, the three Islanders saw the hideous painted masks and perfect armor and sharpened weapons that they themselves had made for the River people.

Some of the Inland warriors shouted to each other; they expressed great wonder, unable to believe that such a little canoe would dare to come against them. The warriors of the

River people stared with fascination at this proud sea king, so unafraid, accompanied only by a poor old one-handed man and a servant boy. Of course, any one of the River warriors imagined that they could have killed them easily, but they did not, for they admired bravery above all other things. Still laughing and shouting above the roar of the river, they turned their big canoes and followed the little dugout to shore. Many of the warriors said that they would give anything to have a son who could paddle a canoe with such skill.

On the bank of the river the five village chieftains sat on beautifully carved boxes and waited. They were proud that all the Inland clans had gathered together to slaughter these outrageous Islanders, these sea beasts, these traitors whom they used to call their friends.

Even with the paddle's help it took all of Hooits' strength and cleverness to land the little dugout canoe in front of the five chiefs. Behind him, Hooits could hear the warriors joking. They easily worked their large canoes toward the beach, showing little concern for the power of the river.

Hooits stared at the most mighty Inland chief, the one who sat in the very center, wearing white ermine tails so long that they trailed to the ground. His dark eyes were protected by the huge hooked bill of his Eagle mask. A white bone pin driven through his nose gave him the fierce snarling look of a mountain lion.

This chief raised his hand and signaled to an almost naked slave, a huge mountain man they had captured in the north

country. Hooits had often heard stories of this gigantic slave. His neck was as thick as a man's waist, and the top of his father's head would only have come to this giant's chest. It was said that he was sometimes as cruel as a wildcat playing with a half-killed rabbit and that his muscles were so thick beneath his skin that ordinary blows could not harm him. It was said that when this giant caught hold of a man, he would toss him in the air like a bear throwing up a salmon; then he would hold out the side of his immense hand in such a way that when the man fell against it, his back would be broken.

Obeying the chief's signal, this giant of a man took up an immense whalebone war club carved in the shape of a killer whale. He slung the huge club onto his shoulder and strode down the beach, eager to show off his tremendous strength, eager to slaughter the foolish chieftain of the sea raiders. He also could not believe that this Island chief would have dared to come here without warriors.

Hooits sat in speechless terror as the giant mountain man stood towering over his father. Hooits could hardly believe that his father would risk his life in such a way while trying to make peace with these River people.

The huge slave hesitated, not knowing what to do. He expected this sea raider either to leap out fighting or to cringe like a dog. When neither happened, he waited. He wondered whether he should simply club this brave old white-haired chief, who sat unmoving before him, straight and proud, or

43

whether he should drag him out of the canoe and haul him up to kill him at the feet of the Eagle chief.

Hooits watched the mountain man's face as he tried to decide. Slowly his huge forehead creased, his sharklike eyes grew cruel, his neck muscles tightened. He raised the whalebone club high above his head. Hooits knew he had to act now or never.

Hooits leaped up in the canoe. He held only the short ghost paddle. He felt it singing in his hands. Hooits swung the paddle with all his might and slashed out with its sharp tip at the giant's throat.

The mountain man, huge though he was, was well trained and quick as a fox. He lunged backward, just saving himself from the cutting stroke. This retreat gave Hooits the instant he needed to leap from the canoe.

Wasco, the Sea Wolf, sat wide-eyed with surprise, for he had never thought of this young son as a fighter. Not until

this awful moment, when he saw him confronted by the mountain giant, did he realize the courage his son possessed.

Hooits was crouching, weaving sideways, holding the sharp delicate paddle before him like a sword.

The warrior-slave eyed him for a moment like a hawk watching a sparrow. He then roared and lifted his mighty club, making it disappear behind his back. He brought it downward with one great smashing blow, a deadly stroke that would have broken Hooits in half. But because the giant expected Hooits to dodge to the right or left, the giant stopped the whale club in mid-flight, then sent it ripping sideways through the air in a tremendous circle at the height of Hooits' waist.

Wasco could not believe that his untrained son could have been waiting and expecting this very stroke. All too well Wasco knew this classical fighting trick often used by the mountain warriors. He felt a surge of pride when he saw his son, Hooits, the one who had never fought, leap into the air, escaping the swing of the deadly club that whistled just beneath his naked toes.

While in the air, Hooits saw the giant's wrists exposed before him. The Grizzly spirit in him needed only this one chance. He slashed downward with the sharp edge of the ghost paddle. He heard it scream like an eagle, and when it struck its prey, the blade splintered into many pieces.

The giant shrieked as the mighty club fell from his hands. He rolled on the ground, groping madly to regain the heavy weapon, lashing out with his feet at Hooits, who had also stumbled and fallen.

Wasco, the Sea Wolf, howled with pleasure at the wild sight of such a battle. But this was enough. Now he, too, leaped from the canoe and landed with both feet on the huge war club.

Seeing the swift action of this bold chieftain and watching Hooits spring to his feet once more, with the broken paddle held in his hands like a weapon, the giant recognized the pair. Holding his wrists, his face a mask of pain, he cried out, "Wasco! Wasco! It can only be the Sea Wolf and his son."

The chiefs and all the people called out, saying, "Yes. Yes. It is surely Wasco's son, the Sea Wolf's son dressed as a simple paddler. That is why he has beaten the mountain giant, for who else would fight like that?"

Wasco stepped off the giant's club and, bending, picked it up and handed it to his son. In exchange Hooits gave him the ghost paddle with its splintered blade. His father looked at the paddle for a moment, holding it upright before him, and then said, "Thank you," as though the paddle were a real person. Then Hooits heard him whisper, "Magic paddle, dream vision of mine, you came from the water. I now return you to the water," and holding the paddle like a spear, he flung it far out into the river.

Then Hooits shouted to the Eagle chief, "This club is a weapon of war, and we are here for peace." He whirled around three times and released the great whalebone man killer. It spun out over the river and fell, disappearing into the rushing waters.

"Yes, it is I, Wasco, the Sea Wolf, and my son, Hooits, whom you have never seen, so long have we two been at war. You see that we have thrown away our only weapons. We come to you in search of *peace*."

Wasco could see that the five chiefs were angry because their giant had been so quickly defeated. He saw one of the chiefs secretly signaling to his warriors to attack the three of them as they stood defenseless on the beach.

"Three times· you have been deceived," Wasco shouted, holding up three fingers to the chiefs.

"Believing that my son, Hooits, was a simple paddler is only the third way you have been deceived.

"See this!" he cried, and the old one-handed man, Yahil, whom they knew so well, raised both his arms and waved two hands at the warriors and chiefs.

All the River people gasped in horror. How could any man grow a new hand? Yet there it was, strong and well, with every finger flexing and wriggling. The five chiefs leaped from their seats, crying out in astonishment.

Wasco stood proudly before the rival chiefs and said, "We have come to you as you demanded, only when Yahil has grown a new hand." He paused, then he continued speaking. "That hand is made from wood; its fingers move by pulling strings, like a puppet upside down. It was made and painted by our most famous carver. That is the second way in which you have been deceived.

"But these two deceptions are as nothing compared with

50

the first way in which you were deceived by those fugitive tricksters, those killers, the Gwenhoots. A dozen winters past, when your men were fishing in the darkness on the river, those night raiders came crawling into your camp and stole your women and children. They were careful to leave only our beautifully carved masks and weapons behind, knowing that you would believe that the treachery was ours and seek revenge upon us and cease your precious trade with us. That trickery has kept us apart for all these years."

Then to show that they were without guilt or fear, Wasco, Hooits, and Yahil, with his newly grown wooden hand, walked up and presented a gift box to the chiefs. It was received in silence, as sharp eyes watched their every move.

"I see that you still have doubts," said Wasco. "Still you believe that we may deceive you. But you have watched us come among you, surrounded by our children. We bear no weapons, only gifts wrapped in red trading cloth inside the boxes. We only wish to gather berries and to buy a few of your small candlefish, the oolichan, in exchange for these gifts that we have carried inland for you.

"Yesterday along the river trail we suffered your attack against a prince of the Wolf clan. A sly black feathered arrow flew out of the forest. You have heard us wailing and tearing our clothing for that young prince, but like my son, he, too, lives life.

"Now we must forgive all the old wrongs, for we are eager to resume our friendship and our trade with you. If you need further proof, send your big canoes across this river, and my people will give meaning to the pure truth of my words.

The Eagle chief waved to his boatmen, who then crossed to the opposite bank and returned with two women of the Inland River people. At the river's edge, weeping with joy, the women leaped into the water, so anxious were they to rush up the bank and be among their families, clasp them to their breasts, and feel their husband's and their children's hands again.

"These women have something to say to you," called the Sea Wolf. "Listen to them carefully."

"What Wasco says is true," they both said. "We were stolen from this place by the Gwenhoots who treated us cruelly. These good people who live on the large island beneath the shining mountain got us back from the Gwenhoots in exchange for many masks and weapons. They treated us well, and now they are returning us home again."

Hearing this story, the five chiefs stood to honor the Sea Wolf and his son. Wasco pulled off his rich cape and placed it over his son's shoulders and set the headdress on Hooits' head. Wasco himself stood only in his loincloth, naked as a paddler.

At the Eagle chief's signal, a goat-hair robe of glorious design, all white and blue and black and yellow, was brought and placed around Wasco's shoulders. Its long fringes dangled almost to the ground. A tall hawk's headdress, with ermine tails and red trade cloth and flashing abalone shell, was then gently placed upon his head.

The five River chiefs shouted to the Sea Wolf, saying, "Wasco, we see a mighty chief growing in this son of yours, for did he not have the courage to defend you when that great whale club was about to burst your brains upon the beach? He did not hide from the mountain giant, this son of yours. He rose without a real weapon and fought openly and bravely as becomes a chief's son, and yet he did not kill.

"Return to the other side of the river and rest yourselves," said the Eagle chief. "Tomorrow, when the sun stands high, we will send boats for you and bring all of your party to us. We will prepare a feast for you in thanks for returning these women to us and this one-handed old man to his wife. We now believe that we have wrongly accused you of treachery. Tomorrow we will start our trade with you and give you gifts. Once again we will build good will between us and make an end to war."

The following day the Islanders spent readying themselves for the feast. First they bathed in the river to purify themselves; then each man combed out his hair, letting it hang freely, showing the Inlanders that beneath their hats it was not knotted and pinned with the sharp bone skewers that would stop an enemy from grabbing their hair.

The Inland canoes arrived for them just as the sun was setting, turning the river into a bright stream of gold. All of the Islanders paraded down to the river. The girls were in a state of high excitement, for all of them were young and had never attended a feast except among their relatives at home.

When they reached the Eagle crest house, Wasco was the first to enter. The River people were arrayed in all their finery. The whole great room was brightly lighted with a hundred burning candlefish that gave off a delicious smoky smell, making one think of the great feasts of which they had so often heard.

Hooits proudly followed his father and after him walked Hawn, wearing the hardwood armor across his body, with the Inland arrow still protruding from the center of his chest.

When they stopped before the places of honor that the Inlanders had arranged for them, they paused, and Wasco gave a signal. Hawn reached up and pulled the black-feathered arrow from his chest and drove it into the ground before the fire. Wasco then flung a handful of eagle down into the air as a sign of peace.

All the voices of the Inland River people rose in a joyful chorus. A moment later some of the roof boards were pulled away, and the eagle down of peace filled the air like snow. A boy clinging to the ridge pole poured rich oil down onto the fire, causing it to blaze up with a bright white flame. Splendid gifts were passed out by the River people, and in turn the Islanders gave out their treasures of beautifully carved horn spoons, rattles, drums, and wind flutes.

In all the pleasure and confusion, Hooits had not noticed one particular Inland girl. He was not supposed to have seen her, for she had been sitting half hidden in the shadows. But now with the coming of the second part of the feasting, servants rushed forward and surrounded her with light.

Hooits had never seen any girl so young and yet so sure of herself. She sat high on a pile of treasures: great carved chests and white bearskins and red trade blankets and huge, priceless copper coins belonging to her father. On her head she wore the carefully carved frontlet of the Hawk, and around her neck she wore a heavy necklace of eagle claws and abalone shells. On her arms were wide, thick bracelets beaten from the gold and silver coins of the bearded sea traders. She sat erect, her back as straight as an arrow. Her face was beautiful; her hair was blue-black and shiny as a raven's wing. But most noticeable of all were her large dark eyes that stared straight at Hooits.

She stood up, holding his ghost paddle in her hands.

"Come," she called to Hooits. "Take it. This paddle is yours. See, we have mended it with a band of silver hammered by our finest craftsmen. Come, take what is yours."

The wind flutes then sounded four high notes, and this Inland princess began her singing:

> "See me, O chief's son.
>> I am a princess born of noblemen.
>> My father possesses a fortune.
>> I am seated on many coppers,
>> I have many names and privileges,
>> I have canoes and masks and dishes.
>> Who shall feast with me? Who?"

This princess of the Eagle clan had sung her song so boldly that Hooits turned his head and looked at Kaws-Kaws to see if he could read her thoughts. Immediately he could tell that Kaws-Kaws was jealous of this boastful song, for she stood stiffly staring at this Inland girl.

Suddenly the room darkened and the drumming began again. A woman screamed like a mountain spirit, and the long-billed, masked Wha Wha birds began their weird dancing, whirling in their great bark capes. After them came a clown who made everyone laugh. When he was finished, it was the time for feasting.

3

The Eagle chief clapped his hands, and a carved wooden dish as long as a small canoe was carried in by six strong men. It steamed in the night air, giving off a delicious odor of river trout and the eggs of snipe, and cranberries and young seaweed all mixed together with the delicate oil of oolichan. Hooits and Kaws-Kaws had never tasted such food in all their lives.

This was followed by the rich red haunches of young mountain goats and saddles of deer meat and the thick warm breasts of sea ducks and fat winter geese and the soft tails of beaver.

Both Hooits and Kaws-Kaws and all the others wished that this feast would never end. But finally the Inland chiefs rose, one by one, and spoke, each saying in a different way that they rejoiced, knowing peace had truly come.

The last one said, "You are soon to return to your island home where you will tell your people that together we have put an end to war. When the winter moons return, we will rejoice in seeing your people come once again and share a potlatch with us.

"We beg you to send your finest carver here long in advance of your coming, so that he may carve a totem for us with our family crests of Eagle, Raven, Wolf, and Bear. We will repay you with boxes of candlefish beyond counting."

All the people sang out their approval:

"Skyspear, Skyspear,
rising, rising.
Crests of Raven,
Eagle, Wolf, and Bear,
rising, rising,
up against the evening sky."

Hooits saw that Kaws-Kaws was singing with all the others. She looked at her brother and smiled; her anger was gone.

Many servants again ran forward and held lights around the Inland princess. Standing up, she took Hooits and Kaws-Kaws by the hands in a gesture of friendship and led them to the entrance. They were followed by Wasco and the Eagle chief and all the other noblemen according to their rank. The princess did not leave her father's house, but stood in the entrance and watched as the long procession of Islander and Inland people walked together down toward the river, carrying a hundred oil-soaked torches to light their way.

As Wasco and the other chieftains stood talking near the canoes, Hooits saw the flaming torches darting up and down the dark beaches and heard the young people running and laughing and singing out to each other. For the first time in their lives they had nothing to fear. The night was clear and the sky was bright with stars and the moon reflecting down the whole length of the river.

"I shall return to this place," thought Hooits, "when winter comes again. Joined together, we shall raise a Skyspear, a great totem pole with all our family crests entwined."

As he stood watching the white mountains glowing in the moonlight, he heard a sound somewhere up in the tall trees near the Eagle house. It was a wind flute echoing softly, sending its low haunting notes up to the stars. Hooits felt the silver-bound paddle trembling in his hands. Had its ghostly markings changed all their lives?

Slowly the feeling of peace came to him, the first that he had ever known. Peace seemed to come and wrap itself gently around him, like a warm cloak protecting him, protecting all of them against the killing winds of war.